This Book Belongs To:
Kaitlyn Nicole Hopkins
11/89

The Muppet Babies live in a nursery
in a house on a street that is a lot like yours.
But they can travel anywhere anytime using a special power—
the power of the imagination.
Can you imagine what it would be like to go with them?
Join the Muppet Babies on this adventure and find out.

Weekly Reader Presents

Meet the Muppet Babies

By Louise Gikow • Illustrated by Lauren Attinello

Muppet Press/Marvel • New York

This book is a presentation of
Weekly Reader Books.

Weekly Reader Books offers book clubs for children
from preschool through high school.

For further information write to:
Weekly Reader Books
4343 Equity Drive
Columbus. Ohio 43228

Weekly Reader is a trademark of Field Publications.

Printed in the United States of America

Baby Kermit was sitting on the nursery floor. He had a big cardboard box and was busy cutting a hole in it.

"What a great cave!" said Baby Fozzie, coming over for a look.

"Just imagine," Fozzie went on. "A bear could tell jokes in this cave all winter long."

"Bears hibernate in the winter," Kermit said. "They sleep until the weather gets warm again. They don't tell jokes."

"They sleep all winter because they're bored,"
Fozzie explained. "If I told them jokes, they'd laugh all
winter."

"Anyway," Kermit added, "this isn't a cave. It's a—"
But Fozzie had run off to get some warm clothes so
the bears in his cave wouldn't freeze.

"Wow!" said Gonzo, who had wandered over to look at the big box. "What a terrific space station! Those must be Martians."

"It's not a space station," said Fozzie. "It's a—"

But Gonzo ignored him. "Now what it really needs," he went on, "is a fleet of rocket-powered spaceships. Then I can travel into outer space. I can even get some milk for my cereal from the Milky Way."

"Zoom, zoom, zoom!" Gonzo flew to the Milky Way in his spaceship. He borrowed the Big Dipper to carry some milk back to the space station. He got there just in time for breakfast.

That's when Scooter came by.

"Terrific!" he called out. "You're building a giant computer! But where's the keyboard?"

"Huh?" said Gonzo. "This isn't a computer! It's a—"

But Scooter had already gone to get his alphabet blocks. He wanted to build a computer keyboard.

"Isn't it fantastic?" asked Scooter. "This is the biggest computer in the world! It can figure out anything, including how to add a million billion and a zillion trillion!"

"What a neat piano!" said Rowlf,
coming over to see what was happening.

"It's not a piano!" Scooter said. "It's a—"
But Rowlf had already sat down to play.

Rowlf began to play his favorite song, "How Much Is That Doggie in the Window?" in the key of G. When he was finished, the audience stood up and cheered.

"I wish the rest of the orchestra were here," he thought. So he went to find them.

"A parade!" Skeeter sang out when she saw
what Rowlf was doing. "With a marching band
and everything!"

"It's not a parade," Rowlf insisted. "It's a—"
Skeeter interrupted him. "I'm going to get my
baton!" she shouted.

"Ta-brum, brum, brum. Ta-brum, brum, brum!"
Skeeter marched up and down Main Street, twirling
her baton.

"What a lovely castle," Piggy said, coming over.
"Look at the moat and all the towers. Where's the
handsome prince?"

"It's not a castle," said Skeeter, forgetting her baton, which fell and hit her on the toe. "Ouch! It's a—"

But Piggy was already imagining herself at the royal ball.

She was wearing a beautiful pink gown and dancing to her favorite song. Her partner was a handsome prince.

"Jungle!" Animal yelled, clapping his hands. "River!"
Baby Piggy stamped her foot. "Jungle? It is not a
jungle. It's my beautiful castle!"

But Animal had already run off. He came back with
three plants and a paddle.

"Animal ride boat!" he said. Then he put his canoe in the water and paddled away.

Just then, Nanny walked into the nursery.

"What is that?" she asked, looking at all the things
on the floor.

"Jungle!" Animal growled, sailing down the river.

"It's a castle, Nanny!" said Piggy, twirling around.
"And I'm the beautiful princess!"

"No. It's a parade!" Skeeter insisted, picking up her baton.
Rowlf shook his head and said, "It's a piano and an orchestra."

"It's a giant computer," Scooter piped up. "I've just asked it how to make chocolate pudding."

"It's a space station on Mars!" shouted Gonzo. "Blast off!"

"It's my very own Comedy Cave," said Fozzie. "Have you heard the one about the sleeping bears?"

"It isn't any of those things!" Kermit finally yelled. "I started it, and I should know!"

Nanny laughed. "Well, Kermit," she said. "What is it?"

"Gee, Nanny," said Kermit, scratching his head. "I don't remember anymore."

Can **you** imagine what it might be?